The Pond

This book belongs to

_____

_____

_____

For my dear friend Valerie.
Cathy Fisher

For Eva John with love.
Nicola Davies

The Pond, first published in hardback by
Graffeg Limited 2017.

Paperback edition first published by Graffeg in 2018.
Author Nicola Davies, illustrator Cathy Fisher, design
and production Graffeg Limited copyright © 2017.

Nicola Davies is hereby identified as the author of this
work in accordance with section 77 of the Copyrights,
Designs and Patents Act 1988.

A CIP Catalogue record for this book is available from
the British Library.

ISBN 9781912213504

1 2 3 4 5 6 7 8 9

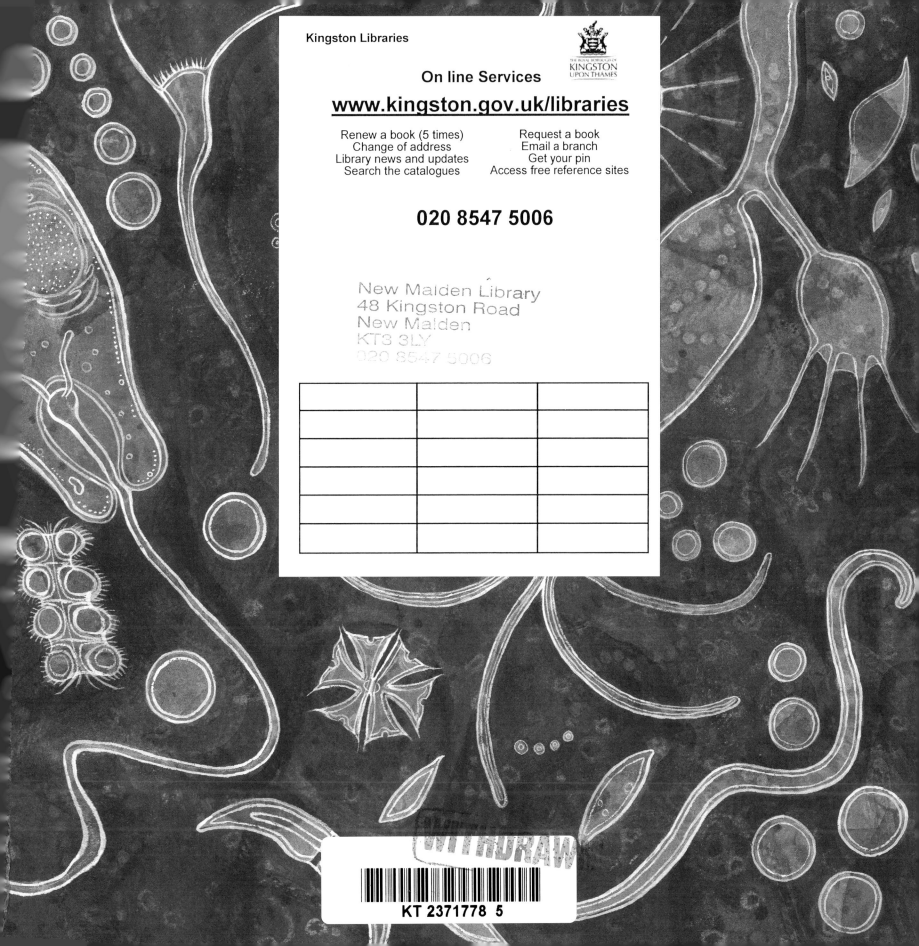

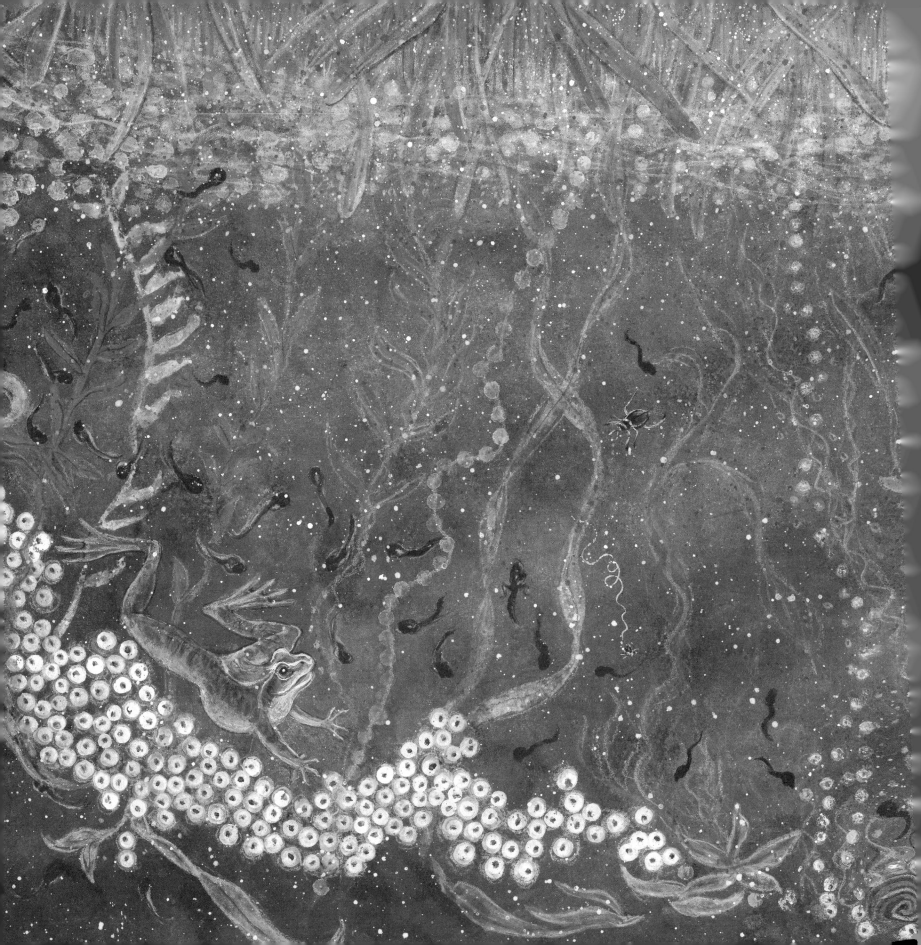

The Pond

Nicola Davies

Illustrations Cathy Fisher

GRAFFEG

Dad talked a lot about the pond.
"There will be tadpoles," he said, "and dragonflies."
Mum told him that our garden was too tiny and
my brother said that ponds were gross and stinky.

Dad took no notice.
He just smiled and whispered,
"Wait until you see the water lilies!"
"Will there be ducks?" I asked.
"Oh yes!" he said, "Of course
there will be ducks!"

Dad never got his tadpoles or his dragonflies.
He died and left a muddy, messy hole that filled
our garden.

Dead leaves blew in, tin cans, all sorts of rubbish.
Ugly weeds grew tall.

We all stared out at it: the muddy, messy hole
that filled our hearts.

And then, one early, early morning
I heard quacking.

A duck had landed in the bottom of the hole.
It quacked on and on and on.

I put my coat on over my pyjamas and went outside.

The duck just went on quacking.

So I got the hosepipe from the shed and poked it through the window to the kitchen tap.

Water splashed in around the duck and made a puddle that grew and grew and grew...

The duck began to swim,
and for a moment I could hear Dad's voice
telling me about the tadpoles.

But the pond edge broke, the duck flew off and all the water ran into the house.

I'd never seen my Mum so angry. She shouted that I'd made the mess much worse. My brother woke and he yelled too.

Mum said that she would get the hole filled in so you couldn't tell that anyone had ever tried to make a pond.

I ran upstairs into my room
and screamed and screamed
at Dad for dying.

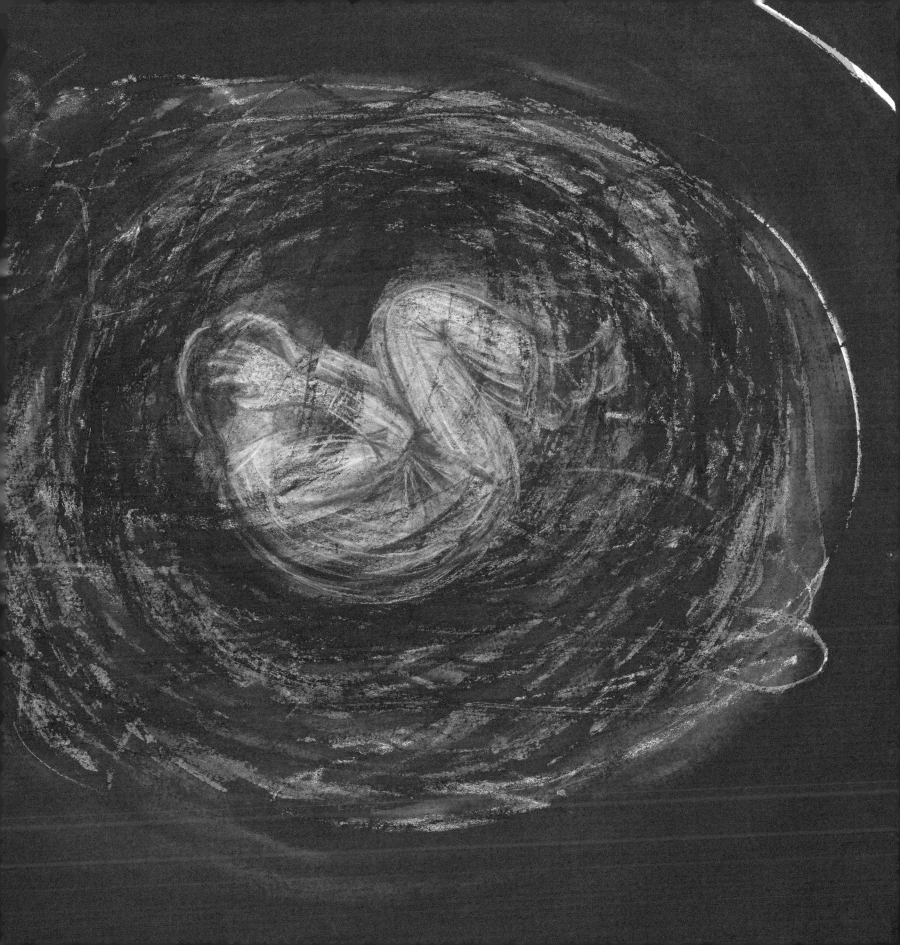

After that, the days limped on. Mum went to work; we went to school. We ate dinner, slept, got up again. The mud around the pond froze solid. Frost killed the weeds. Everything was dark and cold.

Then, one afternoon when we got home,
the pond had got a neat new edge
and the hole was lined with plastic.

Mum said that we could fill it up.
My brother didn't want to,
so I turned on the tap and held the hose.

I closed my eyes and tried to hear Dad's voice
telling me about the water lilies but all I heard
was traffic grumbling along the road.

The pond was just a hole with water in it.

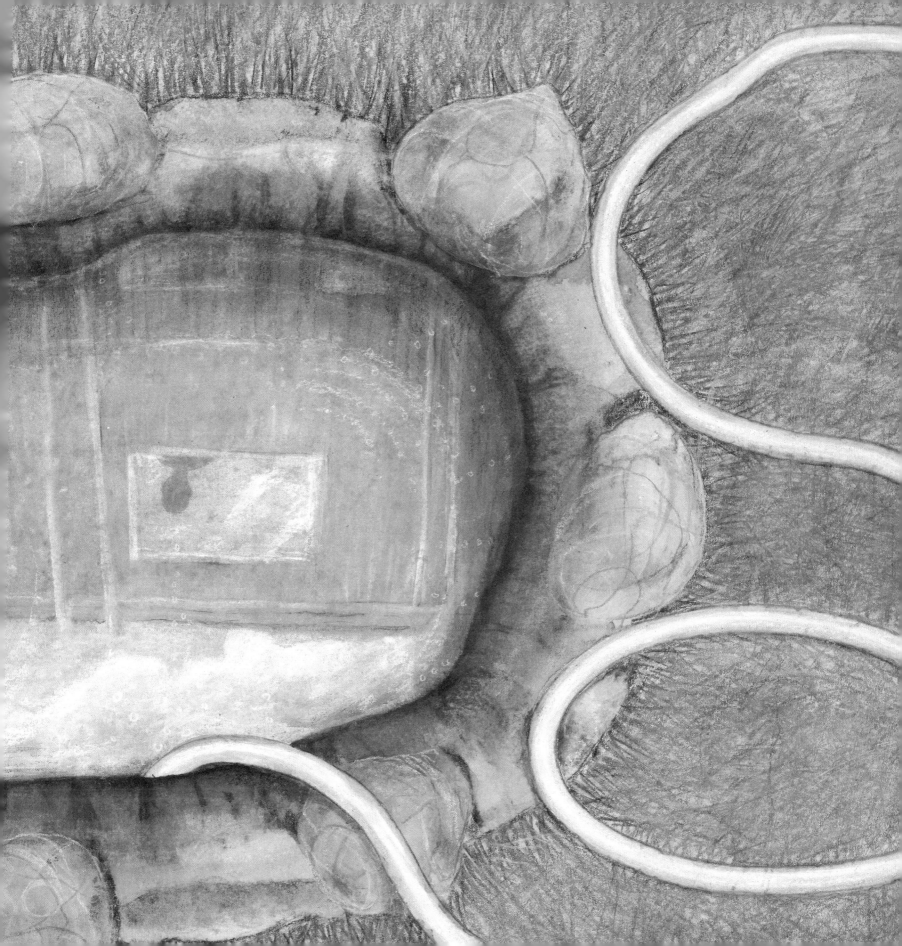

My brother was the
first to see the change.
He was poking at a
floating tin can with a stick.
"Look!" he said, "There's
something moving!"
I couldn't see into the water,
so I got my swimming goggles.
My brother laughed.
"You're mad," he said.
But then he went and got his goggles too,
and we both looked underwater.

It was amazing.
Underneath the floating rubbish,
behind a blanket of green grunge,
our pond had come to life.

Beetles dived with silvery beads of air caught on their legs. Tiny snails clung on green tendrils. And there were tadpoles, just like Dad said that there would be.

Mum found us by the pond when she got back from work. She got Dad's old snorkel from the shed and she looked too.
"I think I found a newt!" she said.

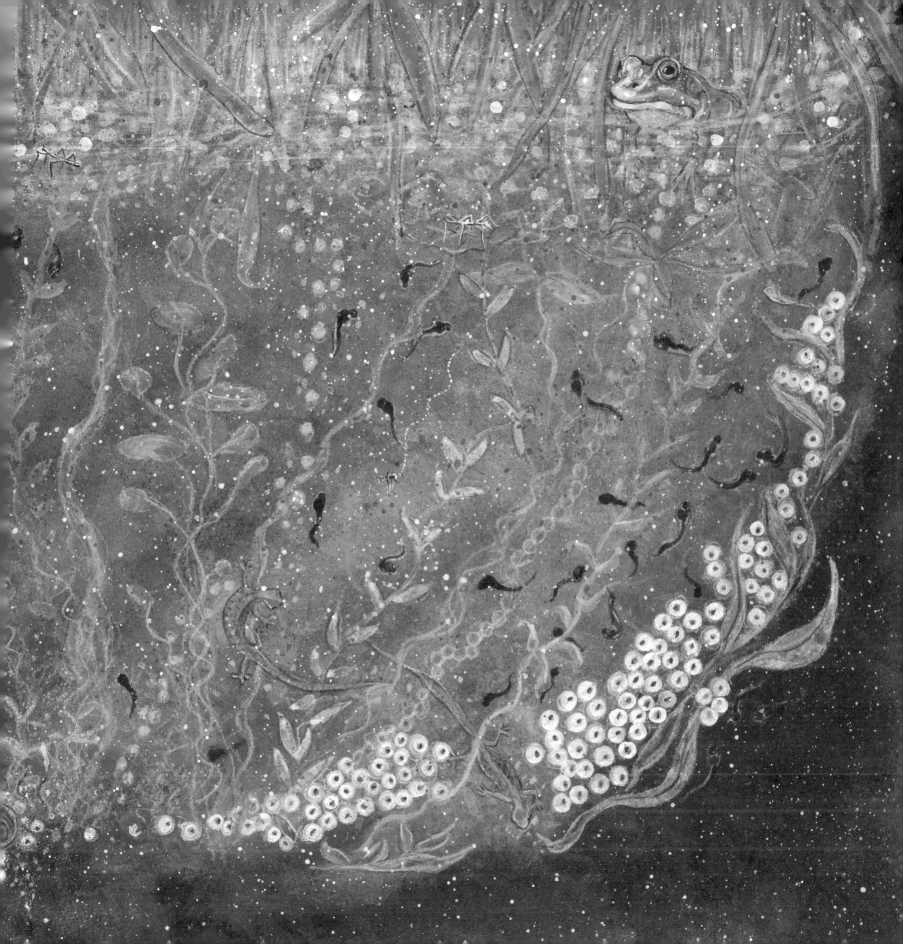

Letter for daddy.
I miss you Dad
I have been feeling
sad
Your pond is not a
black hole any more.
The muddy mess is
tidy now
The ponds got new
life. I hope you
can see it in the
sky with the stars
that shine like you do

Pond Plan Key: Plantings.
1. Cardamine Pratensis
2. Hippuris Vulgaris
3. Iris Pseudecorus Native
4. Lily
5. unknown
6. unknown
7. Hippuris Vulgaris
8. unknown
9. Pond Weed
10. Pond Weed
* Must check that submerged
plants like Lily have not been
knocked over in pots.
* Buy net in Autumn to put over
pond to stop leaves falling in.

OUR ~~MUMMYS CAKE~~ DRAGON FLY

OUR POND
PLAN

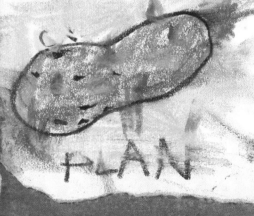

THE OBSERVER'S BOOK
OF
POND LIFE

POND LIFE

List of things we've seen in the
Pond so far:
1. eggs and spawn.
2. tadpoles.
3. tiny frogs
4. Adult frog
5. slime
6. weeds
7. snails
8. beetles
9. dragonfly
10. mosquitos
11. pond skaters
12. water boatman
13. spiders
14. damselflies
15. newts (and eggs and tadpoles)
16. unidentifiable tiny creatures
17. lots of leaves and bits of rubbish.
18. darting flies (caddis?)

(Dad's original plan)

After that, we were always
looking in the pond.

Mum made a cake to celebrate the
first time we saw a dragonfly.
And on my birthday my brother
got me a water lily plant.

P.T.O.

1st LIKLY

HAPPY BIRTHDAY

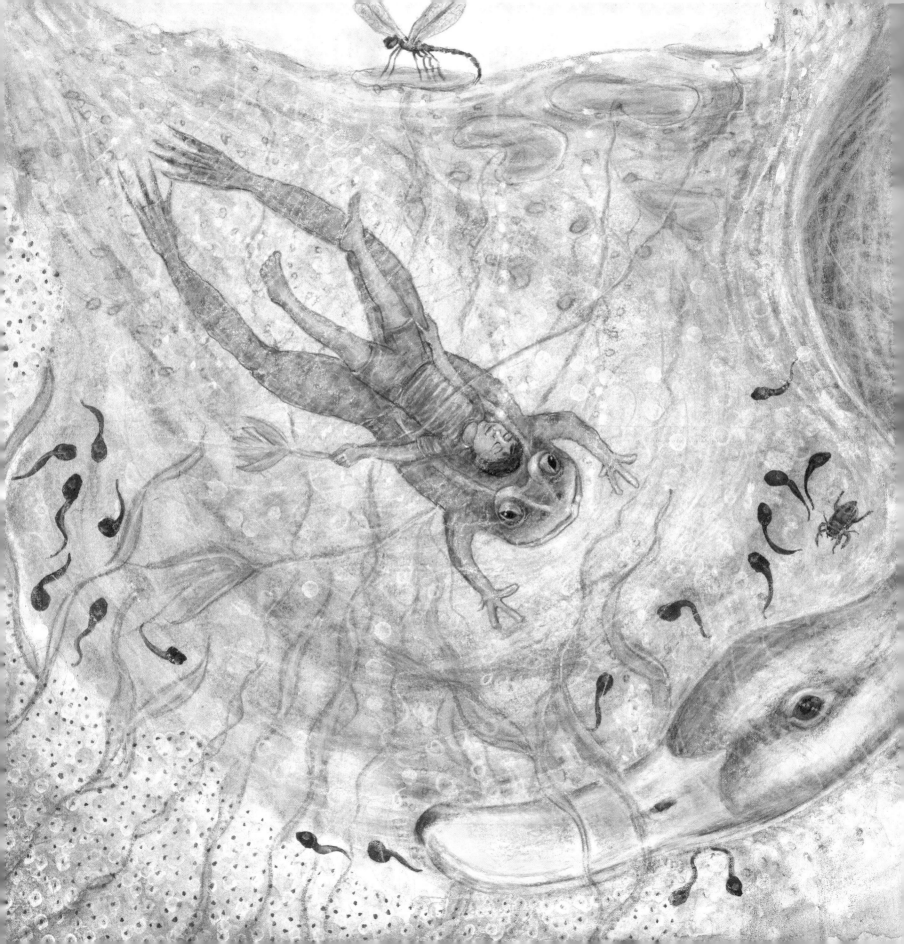

Sometimes, I'd sit beside the pond
and tell Dad all about it.

The tadpoles and the dragonflies, the
snails and beetles and pond skaters.

I had to break it to him that it wasn't
really big enough for ducks to live on.

But he was right about the water lily.
It spread its leaves like stepping stones
then it put out four big fat buds...
and on the day that we moved house,
at last they opened.

"Just you wait until you see the water lilies."

It was time to leave, to say goodbye.
We got into the car and for a long
time no one spoke.

And then Mum said,
"The first thing that we'll do in our
new house is build a pond."

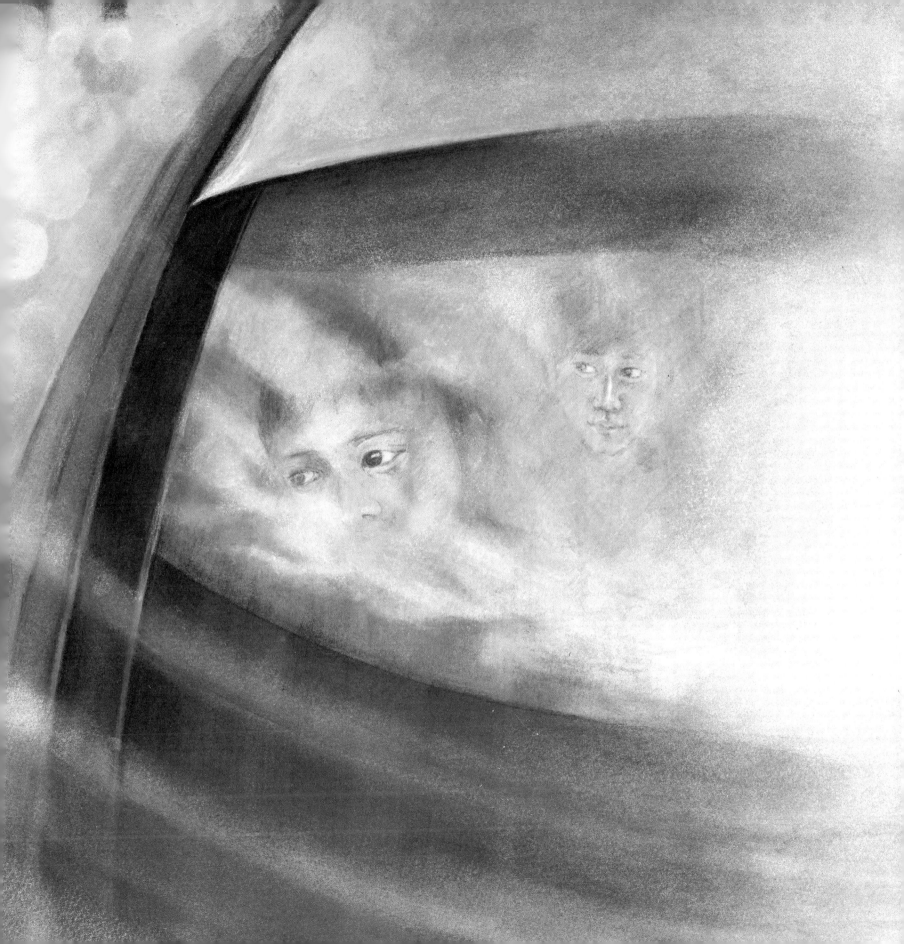

Nicola Davies

Nicola is an award-winning author, whose many books for children include *The Promise* (Green Earth Book Award 2015, Greenaway Shortlist 2015), *Tiny* (AAAS Subaru Prize 2015), *A First Book of Nature*, *Whale Boy* (Blue Peter Award Shortlist 2014), and the Heroes of the Wild Series (Portsmouth Book Prize 2014). She graduated in zoology, studied whales and bats and then worked for the BBC Natural History Unit. Underlying all Nicola's writing is the belief that a relationship with nature is essential to every human being, and that now, more than ever, we need to renew that relationship.

Nicola's children's books from Graffeg include *Perfect*, *The Word Bird*, *Animal Surprises*, *Into the Blue* and the Shadows and Light series: *The White Hare*, *Mother Cary's Butter Knife*, *The Selkie's Mate and Elias Martin*.

Cathy Fisher

Cathy Fisher grew up with eight brothers and sisters, playing in the fields overlooking Bath. She has been a teacher and practising artist all her life, living and working in the Seychelles and Australia for many years. Art is Cathy's first language. As a child she scribbled on the walls of her bedroom and ever since has felt a sense of urgency to paint and draw stories and feelings which she believes need to be heard and expressed. *Perfect* was Cathy's first published book, followed by *The Pond*.

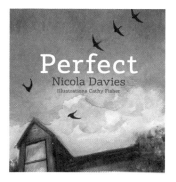

Perfect
Author Nicola Davies
Illustrator Cathy Fisher
ISBN 9781910862469
Published by Graffeg

Resources

Download and print helpful resources to aid teaching *The Pond* and other Graffeg children's titles in schools: www.graffeg.com/teacher-resources/